STEPHEN WILTSHIRE'S
AMERICAN DREAM

Also by Stephen Wiltshire

DRAWINGS
CITIES
FLOATING CITIES

STEPHEN WILTSHIRE'S
AMERICAN DREAM

STEPHEN WILTSHIRE

MICHAEL JOSEPH
LONDON

MICHAEL JOSEPH LTD
Published by the Penguin Group
27 Wrights Lane, London W8 5TZ
Viking Penguin Inc., 375 Hudson Street, New York, New York 10014, USA
Penguin Books Australia Ltd, Ringwood, Victoria, Australia
Penguin Books Canada Ltd, 10 Alcorn Avenue, Toronto, Ontario, Canada M4V 3B2
Penguin Books (NZ) Ltd, 182–190 Wairau Road, Auckland 10, New Zealand

Penguin Books Ltd, Registered Offices: Harmondsworth, Middlesex, England

First published in Great Britain 1993

Copyright Line drawings © Stephen Wiltshire 1993
Copyright Text © Margaret Hewson 1993

Typeset in Caledonia 10½/13½ pt by Goodfellow & Egan, Cambridge
Colour and mono reproduction by Anglia Graphics, Bedford
Printed and bound in Italy by Amilcare Pizzi, Milan

A CIP catalogue record for this book is available from the British Library.

ISBN 0 7181 3699 3

The moral right of the author has been asserted.

CONTENTS

TO

UNITED AIRLINES

ACKNOWLEDGEMENTS

The Stephen Wiltshire Trust Fund would like to thank United Airlines, to whom this book is dedicated, for their generosity in sponsoring the American trips. Without their cooperation, this book could not have been realised. In particular, Linda Chamberlain and John Beauchamp's infinite patience with our changing schedules was much appreciated.

We are most grateful to the following hotels which provided complimentary accommodation during our trips and gave Stephen such wonderful attention: Best Western in Chicago, The Four Seasons in San Francisco (especial thanks to Jeff Knollmiller), The Regent Beverly Wilshire in Los Angeles, the Scottsdale Princess Resort in Scottsdale, The Grand Canyon National Park Lodges, and The Pierre in New York.

Our thanks to Artline who supply all Stephen's pens; to Wookey Hole Caves Ltd for providing paper; the United States Travel and Tourism Administration for finding photographs from which Stephen could draw.

For permission to quote from *Dickens* by Peter Ackroyd, thanks are given to Sinclair-Stevenson Ltd. and HarperCollins Publishers Inc.

To the ABC 20/20 film crew: Joe Pfifferling, Bob Brown, Donna and Terry Yando Morrison and colleagues who helped to make Stephen's trip memorable on the West Coast.

Our Arizona trip was organised and sponsored by Nicole Olton of Edswest Event and Destination Services, Scottsdale, Arizona, to whom we owe more than words. To Lovena Ohl and Bill Faust of the Lovena Ohl Gallery, Scottsdale; Verma and Robert Rhodes, our guides in Hopiland; Justin Tso, our Navajo guide in Canyon de Chelly; Pam Hait of Strategies, Suzie Pace at Taliesin West; Warren Fisher, our mentor, guide and driver throughout the desert trip; and Papillon Grand Canyon Helicopters, Pat Henry and Wendy Greer for the complimentary helicopter ride across the Grand Canyon.

And, finally, to all those who provided books, photographs, information and support: Peter Christopherson, Mark Cousins, Richard Davies, Francis Finlay of Clay Finlay Inc., John Fisher, Felix Francis, Bobby Geisler, Dr Bea Hermelin, Thomas Hinde, Ian Hislop, Juri Jurgevics, Joe Marcell, Andrew Martin, Jeff McMullin, Michael Middleton, Dr Neil O'Connor, Brian Richards, John Roberdeau, Lydia Ruth, Stephen Tole and Sara Uffelman.

Introduction

This book fulfils a promise I made to Stephen in 1989. Stephen regards America as his spiritual home and the European tour which culminated in the publication of his third book *Floating Cities* was viewed by him as an overture to the real symphony: 'America, My Favourite'.

Anyone who has ever been fortunate enough to form a relationship with an autistic child savant will know that you cannot betray the trust they place in you. It is a responsibility which is both awesome and enormously rewarding. I had promised to take Stephen to America but only after the completion of *Floating Cities*. In an interview with *People* magazine in the spring of 1991, the journalist, John Wright, asked Stephen if there was anything he wished to add. Stephen replied 'I have waited patiently, so patiently, to be taken to America and now I'm going to Chicago in July.' It was such a moving, heartfelt little speech which perhaps conveyed nothing at all to the journalist, his wife or the photographer who were present but to me it was as powerful as Ruth's words: 'Intreat me not to leave thee, or to return from following after thee, for whither thou goest, I will go.'

It is now known that autism is a pre-birth neurological dysfunction. A cacophany of cant has surrounded the disease for many years, not least of which was the prevalent myth that these children developed withdrawal symptoms as a result of an unfeeling, unresponsive mother, commonly referred to as 'the refrigerator mother'. Emotional trauma was yet another diagnosis, together with the view that these children had been brought into a hostile, alien universe. Nothing could be further from the truth. It is an established medical fact that primary autism is congenital and not acquired.

Stephen, like many other autistic children, was mute as a child. From the age of five years old, he communicated to the world by drawing on scraps of paper. Children normally draw, not what they see but what they know. A classroom of children asked to draw a house will illustrate not an aerial view, not the rear or the side elevation but a simple front view. This is because children draw those normal symbolic forms which are essentially conceptual. Stephen was different. His inability to draw these symbolic forms might suggest that he draws not what he knows but what he sees, although it must be stated that Stephen's early drawings which illustrate two-dimensional representation in three-dimensional space, are symbolic in themselves. His drawings of buildings or cars are not photographic images despite his attempt, particularly with automobiles, to represent graphically what is seen. The psychology of perception is such that the attempt for any artist to reproduce 'what he sees' is, at best, an equivalence.

I should like to suggest, albeit tentatively, that autistic artistic savants 'see' everything without necessarily focusing upon anything in particular. The vision of lesser mortals is unconsciously highly selective. Stephen's powers of observation bear an uncanny resemblance to those of Dickens. Peter Ackroyd, in his biography of Dickens, states: ' . . . and there are many pages in his journalism or fiction where he unveils incidents and passages of his childhood with a clarity which seems extraordinary. It is a point to which he draws attention, all the time emphasising the nature and powers of his observation. "I was a child of close observation," he says: "I look at nothing that I know of, but saw everything . . ." he says again: and he makes the same point in part of the autobiographical fragment he once wrote of his childhood, "Their different peculiarities of dress, of gait, of face, of manner were written indelibly upon my memory." This is the constant refrain – this idea of seeing everything without having to focus upon anything – and there is no need to doubt Dickens' word on the subject. Indeed, throughout his life it is clear that he retained a very strong visual memory so that he could, as it were, effortlessly recall the visual details and elaborations of a scene without necessarily understanding its contents and purpose. It is a rare and strange gift, currently believed by psychologists to be related to obsession (it is sometimes found, for example, in children who are unstable) and one which Dickens was able to harness for the purposes of his creativity, so that there are occasions when a perfectly visualised scene rises out of the context of his writing and takes on a haunting irremediable quality of its own.'

Stephen's visual memory is equally eidetic. Both use this gift creatively, Dickens for literature and Stephen for art. The two illustrations of St Paul's Cathedral highlight the miraculous nature of this memory function. There is a nine-year interval between these two memory drawings, the first being executed in 1982 as part of Stephen's London Alphabet (all the alphabet drawings were stolen from the artist) and the second in the spring of 1991 when Stephen was sixteen years old. In this intervening period, Stephen never produced a further drawing of St Paul's, nor indeed did he return to the cathedral and therefore the second drawing relies on his initial childhood memory of the building. This illustrates, quite categorically, that the initial visit captured the full detail of the building. The first drawing possesses

a delicately fanciful air which is most alluring while the later rendering loses the whimsicality of line to strive for a less imaginative, increasingly realistic depiction. I was so astonished when Stephen showed me this second drawing that I asked him to draw other buildings which I knew he had not revisited since his childhood and the results were similar.

In conversation with David Wepman of the *New York Daily News* in February 1992, Stephen stated that he had never been to Japan (the journalist erroneously understood that he had) but that he could draw Tokyo. I foolishly intervened to suggest that this was not the case, whereupon Stephen, in a triumphantly defiant mood, produced the sketch before our eyes which is illustrated here. He had seen Tokyo on television. However transient the image on the screen, Stephen is able to store it and reproduce it days, weeks, even years later. It is interesting that no attention to detail is given to the cars. When questioned, Stephen said, 'I don't like Japanese cars: just matchboxes, not interesting.'

Many psychologists believed that the development of language and social skills would diminish if not destroy Stephen's artistic abilities. Stephen negates this belief. What further evidence is required of Stephen's inventive, playful mind than this sketch, drawn in St Lucia while visiting his grandmother in the company of his mother and his sister Annette? The acrobatic prowess displayed by the diver and the merry Ardizzone-style fisherman are both figments of Stephen's imagination. The carefree holiday mood is evoked in confident, spontaneous freehand and the overall impression is one of pure, unadulterated enjoyment. If pen and paper had not been to hand on this family holiday, Stephen would have drawn with a stick in the sand. His need to express himself through his drawings is compulsive.

This sketch also gives the lie to *The Boy Who Draws Buildings* – the title of the BBC documentary on Stephen in 1991 which supports the theory that the absence of emotional expression is consistent with the subjects these children depict – in Stephen's case, buildings rather than people. My experience of working with Stephen suggests, on the contrary, that there is a rich, imaginative life within his head where young boys and girls play a central role.

Since 1991, Stephen has been enjoying piano lessons with Evelyn Preston once a week. She discovered that her pupil was pitch perfect (all autistic musical savants are pitch perfect but Stephen is not a musical savant) and she has been able to teach Stephen duets; and accompanying himself on the piano to his own lyrics, she encourages him to sing his favourite songs. Music has developed the differing registers of sadness, joy, pain, loss and pure rhythmic pleasure. Few teachers possess Evelyn Preston's instinctive empathy with children and Stephen is most fortunate to explore a hitherto unknown world with a teacher whose enthusiasm communicates itself like an infectious disease to her willing pupil. It seems to me that play-acting (theatre is too grandiloquent a term), music and art are essential to Stephen's social, emotional, mental and artistic development.

Autistic artistic savants have been known in clinical literature for many years. Gottfried Mind, nicknamed 'The Cats' Raphael', was a mentally handicapped artist whose work was purchased by no less august a patron than George IV whose impeccable judgement contributed in a most formative manner to the Royal Collection as we know it today. Nadia, an interesting case of an autistic savant because she is female (seventy-five per cent of all savants are male) found that her artistic talent diminished as she developed speech. Stephen is the only autistic artistic savant in the world whose work, clinical literature apart, has been recorded and published since his childhood and it represents a unique history of a mysterious, awe-inspiring gift which so far defies understanding. This case-book history becomes an irreplaceable form of science until medical knowledge advances.

The drawings illustrated in this book were executed over a seven-month period in 1991. Three trips to the United States were made, the first to Chicago and Washington, the second to San Francisco, Los Angeles and Arizona, and finally the third trip to New York, this to complete the American dream. As already mentioned, we are forever indebted to the generosity of our sponsors but our special thanks must go to 'the desert saint' – Nicole Olton of Edswest Event and Destination Services, Scottsdale, Arizona, for revealing to Stephen the haunting biblical splendour of the Canyon de Chelly and her tireless energy and devotion to a spectacular Arizona landscape which is the natural glory of America.

CHICAGO

Chicago is the pantheon of modern architecture and the world's most dazzling outdoor museum. This city is chosen as Stephen's first destination because it is the birthplace of the skyscraper and 'Things are always at their best in their beginning' according to Pascal. Our artist's predilections favour soaring verticality and vibrant cityscapes. The world's tallest building, the Sears Tower, is an integral feature of Stephen's internal visual lexicon and it is important to seek what Stephen has already metaphorically 'found'.

His excitement in experiencing the physical reality of Chicago is wonderful to see and leads to his immortal words, 'Chicago is a great city.'

This witty cartoon is drawn during our flight to Chicago. It depicts a rather supercilious English couple (Andrew and myself) accompanied by two exuberant teenagers, Stephen and his sister Annette.

THE TRIBUNE TOWER

Stephen sits diagonally opposite this Gothic tower on North Michigan Street with his pad balanced on his travelling-stool. It is our first morning in Chicago and Stephen's eyes are firmly glued to the passing cars which may explain why the Tribune Tower is suffering from a disability similar to that of the Leaning Tower of Pisa. The tower is slightly tipsy, like Stephen himself who is intoxicated with pure, unadulterated pleasure at seeing 'My Favourite Cars'. He looks up only three times in the course of an hour to glance at the tower and the surrounding buildings. In all, less than a minute is devoted to a visual scrutiny of these structures but Stephen could draw the buttressed tower with his eyes closed, if necessary. Nothing is going to shift his focus from the automobiles that are driving past.

AERIAL VIEW OF THE CHICAGO RIVER LOOKING WEST

In the spring of 1991, prior to our trip to Chicago, my husband Andrew bought Stephen a copy of *The Sky's the Limit – A Century of Chicago Skyscrapers* (Rizzoli, New York) while on a trip to Florida. This handsome book is the bible of Chicago architecture and has provided hours of delight for Stephen. The text is informative, impressively well-researched and essential reading for anyone interested in the aesthetic and commercial development of Chicago from its origins to the present day. The drawing opposite is taken from the photograph illustrated on page 175 of that book.

Stephen's ability to anatomise structures is well known. This pen drawing is a technical *tour de force* but it also displays an imaginative creativity in Stephen's depiction of the receding skyline, majestically suggested by blurred pen strokes. Uncanny accuracy is a hallmark of his work when applied to drawings from photographs. The clock on the Tribune Tower in the photograph stands at 6.30 pm; Stephen's drawing shows the hands at one o'clock. Clearly, the time does not justify such scrutiny.

The photograph was chosen by Stephen himself. He likes aerial views and is inordinately fond of the Sears Tower. The drawing took several days to complete and Stephen is justly proud of it.

Aerial View of Chicago with Lake Michigan

This is a companion drawing to the aerial view of the Chicago River looking west. It is taken from a photograph lent to us by the United States Travel and Tourism Administration.

Lake Michigan shoreline can be seen in the distance and the foreground is dominated by the Chicago river and the Tribune Tower. Several days were required to execute this drawing. Faultless perspective, as ever, and a real sense of the feel of the city is caught in this masterly drawing.

View from the North Side of the Chicago River

After breakfast at the Surf Diner on South Michigan Avenue and 11th Street (see Stephen's cartoon), we take a cab to the centre of town.

For this drawing, Stephen is standing in front of the Wrigley Building, with his drawing-pad balanced precariously on the wall beside the Chicago River. To the left, is the limestone classicism of the London Guarantee and Accident Building on the corner of North Michigan Avenue, behind which rises the refined elegance of the Gothic skyscraper, the Mather Tower on East Wacker Drive. The classically inspired Jewellers Building, now known as 35 East Wacker Drive, with its small domed temples at each corner and large domed pavilion on the upper section which once contained, I tell Stephen, the first internal mechanised parking garage, designed as an integral feature of the original structure. It was closed down after fourteen years of use, in 1940, because the elevators were no longer large enough to hold the new American automobiles. It also has to be said that it was subject to frequent mechanical failure which must have enraged the drivers when the key-operated switchboard failed to deliver their cars. But for 1926, it was a brave new world concept. Stephen is most impressed with this anecdote.

On the opposite side of the river, the Chicago Sun Times Building is dwarfed by Mies van de Rohe's rectilinear brown-tinted glass edifice – the last structure erected before his death. The figure to be seen suspended in animation on the exterior of this building is in fact a flag.

There is a delightful freshness and vigour to this drawing. It is as if Stephen has caught this warm July morning with a slight breeze blowing; he is particularly good at capturing the movement of the water and its reflections.

THE CARBIDE AND CARBON BUILDING

The perfect example of an art deco lobby is the Carbide and Carbon Building of 1929 on North Michigan Avenue. The circumstances in which Stephen executes this drawing are not entirely propitious. The two security guards on duty are both triumphs of negation and we are not allowed to seat Stephen anywhere in this foyer despite my pleas. Our Gandhi-style tactics are simply to lie on the floor and be carried out drawing should this prove necessary. Stephen retreats into a corner, disappearing behind a large plant, and sketches with the speed of light. His winning smile prevents further altercations despite the guards' furtive glances. The cosmic boredom of their expressions is delightfully contrasted to Stephen's eagle eye darting round the lobby.

The pencil sketch is penned and coloured when he returns to England.

It is a truly stylish place and Stephen's drawing reflects this. The detailed ornamentation on the lift doors, the balcony and the ceiling is suggested but much more time, in far more congenial circumstances, would have been necessary to illustrate the full richness of this interior.

ROW OF TOWN-HOUSES, LINCOLN PARK WEST

This row of two-storey, red-brick town-houses has a very special charm, due partly to the terracotta ornamentation and good landscaping. Stephen sits on this tree-lined street and draws the houses from the opposite pavement. It is not architecture that one traditionally associates with Chicago but these houses were designed by Louis Sullivan, founder member of the Chicago School of Architecture and Frank Lloyd Wright's *Lieber Meister*. Domestic architecture is as informative as commercial edifices and Chicago's cultural richness, originality and diversity is as evident in its public as in its private buildings. Note the fenestration in these town-houses. Stephen's drawing illustrates the aesthetic refinement, the charm and the perfectly balanced rhythm of these desirable residences.

By a happy accident, a taxi driver, whose first love is architecture, took Stephen on a magical tour of this area one evening. The Chicago inhabitants are justifiably proud of their city and its heritage, and it is a glowing tribute to its people that they should be thrilled to communicate their enthusiasm to complete strangers. Stephen's statement 'Chicago is a great city' is as much a statement about its architecture as it is about the delightful character of its inhabitants.

THE GARDEN OF 1819 LINCOLN PARK WEST

While Stephen is sketching the Sullivan terrace, I go off to investigate the gardens of the houses in this street. Social proprieties are abandoned as I invite myself into strangers' houses. Walter Wielunski, who is spied in his garden from a side-alley on Lincoln Park West, is accosted because, from the tantalising glimpse of an old garden seat and an urn, this would appear to be a garden that is not manicured. I suggest to Walter that Stephen should draw the rear elevation of the house and the garden to illustrate a dimension of Chicago life that is normally hidden from the tourist. With Annette, Stephen collects his drawing equipment, having completed the street view, and we all repair to this charming patio garden. Old cobblestones pave the entire area. Honeysuckle is interwoven with a vine and belladonna, jasmine sprouts in riotous profusion along one border, together with climbing roses. The urns are planted with petunias. Stephen draws the rear elevation from one of the garden seats. There is a wooden addition to the back of the house which provides an extended roof and an open structure which leads to the base of the building. It could be a set for a Tennessee Williams play. Stephen's drawing has no prior pencil sketch and is drawn with immense confidence, straight into pen. It has the freedom of a Matisse sketch and perfectly catches the quaint nature of this delightfully disordered structure. Stephen does not share my enthusiasm for this house and garden. 'It's OK but I prefer the Empire State Building!'

As it was now getting very hot, we all move to a round table in the garden with a welcome umbrella for shade. Andrew realises that his jacket is missing and I remember that I left it hanging on a tree in the street outside over an hour earlier while Stephen was drawing the Sullivan terrace. The jacket contains all Andrew's credit cards, and his spectacles. I rush off and thankfully find that it is still there, hanging on the branch where I had left it. Lincoln Park West is not Michigan Avenue . . .

I come to think that it is an enchanted street because that evening we return to Walter's house by taxi to give him a copy of Stephen's book *Floating Cities*. The Iranian cab driver waits for us and then takes us to Szechwan House, an excellent Chinese restaurant on North Michigan Avenue. No sooner have we sat down than I realise that I have left Stephen's drawings and my notebooks in the taxi. Ten minutes later the Iranian returns to the restaurant with our belongings. Stephen's magical, delphic presence invariably produces singular acts of generosity and kindness. I was reminded of our Moscow visit in the spring of 1990 when we lost all Stephen's cartridge paper which was impossible to replace in Moscow. Various people told me that I would never see it again but that evening all the drawing pads were returned to our hotel.

CHICAGO THEATER

Andrew, Stephen and I arrive at the Chicago Theater only to find that the entire ground floor is roped off and the management refuses us permission to draw from the central balcony on the mezzanine floor, or indeed to walk around the foyer to select the best view.

The project is not abandoned, despite these constraints, because the lavishness of the interior is in marked contrast to the N. State Street exterior. Stephen squats in front of the box office and draws the interior of the foyer from the only angle possible. The splendid theatricality and architectural fantasy, reflecting the celluloid illusion, has been renovated after many years of neglect. The baroque boisterousness of this magnificent interior – formerly a movie palace – is caught. Pencil and pen shading convey depth and provide movement. Note the deft, suggestive pen strokes to convey the grandeur and richness of the central chandelier.

FALLINGWATER, BEAR RUN, PENNSYLVANIA

Why is this house illustrated in the Chicago section of this book? Before our visit to Chicago, I showed Stephen a book my brother owned and loved as a boy, about Frank Lloyd Wright's buildings, illustrated in colour. Wright's formative years were spent in Chicago and it was our plan to visit Wright's Robie House on the outskirts of the city. We never achieved this and to counteract the disappointment, Stephen decided to illustrate Fallingwater because if any American city has the right to claim Wright as its son, it is Chicago.

Fallingwater is a sensational feat as the house appears to be part of the waterfall itself. Horizontal slabs of reinforced concrete cantilevered out over Bear Run by virtually invisible concrete supports, this building violates all rules relating to the accommodation of structure to site and yet it is a resounding triumph. Wright said to Edgar J. Kaufmann, Sr., for whom the house was built in 1926: 'I want you to live with the waterfall, not just look at it.' In another sense, Kaufmann did, because the roof leaked for years.

Stephen's colour drawing instinctively captures the symbiosis Wright sought and so implausibly, yet thrillingly, achieved. Small wonder that this building has acquired universal recognition and is one of the most memorable houses of the world.

THE ROOKERY

Stephen is diametrically opposite this most elegant office building in South Lasalle Street, seated on his travelling-stool on the pavement as the lunch-time passers-by walk past. The original intention was to draw the spectacular interior courtyard of this building which is an aesthetic triumph. Sadly, this proves impossible as restoration is in progress at present.

The Rookery is both graceful and strong in its design and Stephen sketches it quickly in pencil. The ornament is of considerable interest on this building, and architectural features, such as the place where a capital might be found on the columns, are simply emphasised. It suggests a mirroring of the entire design – articulated base, vertical shaft and decorated capital – which is characteristic of Chicago architecture at this time.

Stephen is longing to go to the top of the Sears Tower which we had discussed earlier in the day. 'I'll just finish now because we'll go to the Sears building, Margaret.' This is both a question and a statement but it is understood that I will accept it as a statement. The drawing is not finished but he says, 'I'll do it later from memory.' We pack up and Stephen strides off leaving us to collect his stools and drawing equipment. The Sears Tower is like a magnet to him.

The colossal disappointment of the panoramic view from the roof of the tower is in violent contrast to his anticipated delight and excitement at the prospect while he was drawing the Rookery. He adores aerial views but had not realised that his view would show a scale so small to the eye that it would be rendered virtually meaningless. A hidden bonus, however – it saves us a trip to the top of the Hancock Tower! Stephen is not going to be bitten twice, and consoles himself by buying postcards of the building.

CHICAGO TEMPLE BUILDING

Our party is joined by Joe Pfifferling, the producer of Stephen's documentary for ABC 20/20. Stephen's portrait likeness of him was executed the previous evening during dinner.

Stephen is seated on his travelling-stool in the piazza and sketches the Chicago Temple Building in pencil. It is an unusual marriage of commerce and divinity as the twenty-one-storey office block, built in 1922-23, is capped by an eight-storey Gothic spire which contains a 1500-seat chapel: a Cathedral of Commerce as it were. It is the tallest church in the world today and looks splendidly comfortable in its commercial environment on West Washington Street. Building height restrictions were in force in Chicago while this edifice was in the process of construction. The architects had allowed for the eight-storey spire to be detachable if planning permission was not granted. It wasn't – but the spire remained despite much controversy.

Stephen's figures in the drawing give a sense of the scale of these buildings. How many children would be prepared to illustrate all those windows? Stephen is meticulous where detail is concerned and every single window pane is drawn. The sculpture in the foreground is by Joan Miró.

N. State Street from Bart's Bar and Grill

Our party repairs to Bart's Bar and Grill. There are tables and chairs set for lunch outside but all are empty because the temperature is 100°F and only mad English dogs sit outside at midday. Stephen does not wish to be seated inside – like the sensible Americans – because this would deprive him of his street entertainment: spotting the cars and fire-engines on N. State Street. The Scottish waiter, Brian Doherty from Easterhouse, alters the angle of the umbrella at our table to provide maximum shade.

After a splendid lunch, Stephen moves to the waiter's own table – the sole table in relative shade – which Mr Doherty kindly vacates so that our artist can draw the street scene. The choice presented is either the view to Stephen's right which would illustrate the Carson Pirie Scott department store or the view to the left, as illustrated. The department store is classic Chicago School of Architecture design: wide windows and narrow piers which express the steel frame, finely proportioned with a firm emphasis to the surrounding mouldings, but Sullivan's architecture is abandoned in favour of soaring verticality and the overground railway, known as the 'L'. Few cities would have the audacity or sheer inventiveness to construct a railway above street level around a city. Chicago's confidence and effrontery is wonderfully rewarded because it works.

Stephen is very partial to this drawing and he often singles it out for special attention. It expresses his love of urban life, the bustle of an exciting city and the huge diversity of life it contains. Passers-by sit down to chat to him although unwittingly they obscure his view of the passing cars and he is decidedly regal as he waves his hand to suggest that they move. Stephen's eyes never leave the passing cars, and at frequent intervals he shouts out 'Chrysler Dodge Monaco 1970, Cadillac Fleetwood' and snatches up his camera to immortalise the passing car.

Before we leave Bart's Grill to spend the afternoon in the Chicago Art Museum, Stephen suffers an attack of 'automobile fever'. This is defined as an excess of car mania which cannot be relieved until he has produced a car drawing. The catharsis is achieved by drawing this imaginary Buick against an imaginary Chicago skyline (but note the ubiquitous Sears Tower). His spirits are restored and he is ready to depart.

Our visit to the Chicago Art Institute produces a wonderful reproduction of Edward Hopper's *Night Hawks* which Stephen loved (*see* picture overleaf).

THE CHICAGO SKYLINE

One evening, we walk over to the John G. Shedd Aquarium which is situated on South Lake Shore Drive. It is a rather menacing environment in the evening but we all want to see the city's skyline from this vantage point. As we sit on the grass fending off the young men who wish to engage Annette's attention (I have assumed the role of a despotic duenna for this evening), Stephen, who is blithely unaware of these extramural activities, sketches the boats which are moored in the bay in front of us, and then draws the Chicago skyline. This is rather an achievement because there is a haze hanging over the entire city and it is particularly difficult to discern the structures with any clarity. What had presented itself as an outline of the city's landscape on our arrival has now transformed itself into contours because of the mist that has descended. Clearly, this is not an obstacle as far as Stephen is concerned.

STEPHEN AS A BEVERLY HILLS COP

Not wishing to prolong our visit to the Aquarium beyond what is strictly necessary, we walk back to a hotel on North Michigan Avenue where we all partake of a spectacularly emetic dinner served by America's most loquacious waiter (a glossectomy would have been a kindness). Stephen removes a tattered piece of card from his breast pocket – a card usually referred to as 'The Holy Grail' – on which he has drawn an American automobile and glued a colour photograph (cut out of a magazine) of Jennie Garth, an actress in the American television series entitled *Beverly Hills 90210*. We may ostensibly be a party of four but the phantom fifth presence is Jennie Garth, who appears with unfailing regularity at meals, is attached to drawings while they are being executed, is produced in taxis, and is Stephen's source of delight and inspiration throughout this trip. Like all successful love affairs, she is silent and never met in reality.

To counteract the grim cuisine, we invent a game whereby Stephen assumes the role of an American police cop and I, as Jennie Garth, play the part of Stephen's girlfriend. American accents are *de rigueur* for this game.

In our diners' mini-series, Jennie is the archetypal labile female and Stephen creates his own role of the cop who loves Jennie – but the law takes precedence. Stephen's mask is truly revelatory. Jennie is allowed marriage but not babies: 'Oh, come on, Jennie, babies are an economic burden.' (Where *does* he learn this language which one does not hear in normal conversation?) And she is certainly not permitted a dog. The litany of hatred on the subject of dogs is a monologue I have heard before; Stephen, as a child, was once bitten by a dog. An indulgent, paternalistic attitude is applied to Jennie's vagaries of heart when she decides to go off with another policeman. 'You go, Jennie, you go. But you'll be back and I'm always here.' Although Jennie wishes to see more of him at home, Stephen's cop says, 'The law's the law, Jennie. I have work to do. Am I right or am I wrong?' As Jennie singularly fails to understand the importance of his job, Stephen raises his large brown eyes to the ceiling, frowns and slowly shakes his head in despair with a wry smile. It is as if he has always been stoically resigned to the foolishness of females.

As a Cadillac drives slowly up Michigan Avenue outside the hotel, Jennie asks Stephen to choose between herself and the Cadillac. He chooses . . . the Cadillac. We all burst out laughing and the magic of the game is lost. But there is clear evidence that Stephen possesses a rich imaginative life within his head, a perpetual cinematic life with moral choices, aspirations, fears, loves and despair – *and* language which accompanies it.

190 South Lasalle Street

Stephen and his sister have known Ian Hislop, who is working in Chicago for a few days, for three years. Ian is staying at the Drake Hotel which overlooks the shores of Lake Michigan, The drawing illustrated on the next page shows the view from the hotel dining-room. It could be a sketch of the south of France, and Stephen's light touch is well demonstrated in this spontaneous, refreshingly quirky pen drawing.

We all have lunch at the Inter-Continental Hotel, recently refurbished in splendid Egyptian style. During lunch, Stephen asks for a pen. Is he going to draw the interior? In fact, he pulls out the paper bag from the Sears Tower where earlier he had purchased his postcards and proceeds to catalogue all the cars he has seen in Chicago during his trip and includes those he has not seen but would like to photograph. Amateur ornithologists make lists of their sightings. Stephen catalogues his passion: cars of the seventies.

After lunch, we have an architectural tour of The Loop (so called because all roads lead here to converge in an embracing loop) conducted by Ian at a brisk, if not unnerving pace, with Ian and Stephen striding out ahead as Andrew and I trail behind in the heat.

The foyer of 190 South Lasalle Street is opposite the Rookery and has been chosen for Stephen as part of the afternoon's visual treats. This elegant lobby with its marble walls and pilasters which support a gold-leafed barrel vault is sketched in pencil by Stephen and coloured at a later date. The sculpture at the northern end of this spectacular place is Chicago Fugue by Anthony Caro. The lobby's cathedral-like proportions give a splendid dignity and grandeur to the fascinating interior.

WASHINGTON

If Chicago is the jazz age to Stephen, then Washington is plainsong.

It is 105°F at Dulles Airport and completely overcast on our arrival. The humidity is paralysing and such is the eccentricity of our hotel that it has neither television – a disaster so far as Stephen is concerned – nor air-conditioning in the bedrooms. Andrew and I are in terminal decline but Stephen's stamina never falters.

For a boy whose whole life has been a meditation on modern architectural forms and structures, Washington cannot compete with the 'windy city' but Stephen immediately adapts to his new environment and the marbled grandeur of Washington is attacked with gusto.

THE WHITE HOUSE

Washington, unlike the vast majority of capital cities, was created on a chosen site as the centre of government; the honour of 'capital' city did not arise naturally, like London (as a great port) or Paris as the intellectual and commercial heart of France. In a sense, Washington is a factitious creation and Pierre Charles L'Enfant, who designed the city, produced with considerable panache an American Versailles but failed to understand that cities are living organisms and architecture is above all social. L'Enfant's vaulting ambition – a besetting sin of the French if one recalls Beauvais Cathedral where the great vaults of the choir, in the architect's urge to reach the sky, stood as the highest in France at 157½ feet, only to collapse twelve years after it was completed – is responsible for the spaciousness, the sterile grandeur and splendour of Washington as we see it today, but he over-reached himself with the city fathers and was dismissed, to be buried years later in a pauper's grave.

The White House benefits from L'Enfant's masterplan because the residence is a focal point for a complexity of monuments and buildings that retain a certain basic coherence to the image of Washington as a capital city. The Irish architect, James Hoban, originally designed a Georgian country house for the presidential palace and the great virtue of this house lies in its human scale.

Stephen's drawing is taken from a photograph lent to us by the US Travel and Tourism Administration and the charm of this essentially modest house is well conveyed in this pen drawing.

Stephen Wiltshire

GEORGETOWN

This restrained design is also witnessed in Georgetown, which remains Washington's most exclusive and picturesque residential area. It is here that Stephen feels comfortable because the human scale of Georgetown is diametrically opposed to the monumental marbled grandeur of the capital itself. This may appear strange to those who recall Stephen's fondness for Santa Maria della Salute in Venice and his penchant for the epic, imperial style as witnessed in *Floating Cities* but the refinement of his visual perception rarely falters.

The building height restriction which prevails in this city is well illustrated in Stephen's memory drawing executed on his return to London. He does not choose to record the monuments but focuses instead on a typical street.

His favourite view of Washington is The Capitol (*see* page 45) which is a five-minute sketch penned while the rest of us listen to an open-air concert. Few drawings could ever give such pleasure but this little jewel, the composition of which is exquisite, exemplifies Stephen's innate artistry.

THE MONUMENTS OF POTOMAC PARK

Early one morning, we take a taxi to the Potomac Park to draw the LINCOLN MEMORIAL. This pristine, American-style Parthenon dominates the park (a complete 4,000-gallon washdown of the Memorial takes six working days and nights), and Stephen, who is seated in front of the building, sketches with extraordinary speed. He is well-versed in classical language and is able to produce a completed pencil sketch within half an hour. The final pen and shading work takes place later in London.

On both the frieze of the temple and that of the attic frieze appear the names of the states in the Union, together with their admission dates. In Stephen's drawing, these were drawn from memory a fortnight later, on his return to London. Some are illegible but those which can be read are correct. No greater proof is required of this boy's mysterious memory function – a memory which can reproduce details which the majority of us would never have noticed unless informed – and the names were not noted on the original pencil sketch which Stephen executed in front of the building. It reminded me of the day I asked Stephen about a trip we had made together in the north of Scotland a few years earlier. He immediately told me the make of car we had hired at Aberdeen Airport (of course) but also the registration number of the vehicle!

We wander over to the VIETNAM VETERANS' MEMORIAL and sit on the grass under the trees in front of it. It is a most moving tribute to those who lost their lives in South-East Asia and the twenty-one-year-old Yale architectural student, Maya Lin, who deservedly won this national design

Stephen W.

competition, has provided Washington with its most outstanding memorial. The 58,156 names of those who lost their lives are inscribed on the polished black granite wall in chronological order of the date of casualty. The stark simplicity of this noble design is fittingly placed in a quiet area of the park near to the Lincoln Memorial. The entire design provokes a restrained, uncanny, tearful silence as is witnessed by the day-long parade of visitors who are paying homage to their dead on this hot July morning. Even the cyclists, sartorially defined in all-in-one black and pink Lurex, on their mountain bikes, with attached head-phones blaring out reggae music, fail to counteract the noisiest silence of all: the silent scream of the dead.

A bronze sculpture of three soldiers stands nearby but this statue will never possess the force and emotional control of Maya Lin's abstract naked simplicity.

We tell Stephen the background to the American involvement in Vietnam but he does not understand the concept of war. His pacifist nature is alarmed by violence of any kind and, unlike most boys of his age, he has never shown any interest in war games.

We walk over to the Reflecting Pool and Stephen draws the WASHINGTON MONUMENT as we sit in the shade of a chestnut tree. This pastiche obelisk (it is not a single piece of stone) is in two different colours because work was interrupted by the Civil War for about twenty years and the marble could not be matched. It is the tallest structure in Washington and dominates the city from every angle. From where Stephen is seated, the base is obscured by the foliage of a magnificent weeping willow which softens the thrusting grandeur.

THE SMITHSONIAN INSTITUTION

While sketching the Smithsonian Institution one morning, the master mason in charge of the rebuilding programme here joins us to look at Stephen's drawings. He suggests that we pay a visit to the Cathedral where again he was responsible for the outstanding craftsmanship of the stone sculpture. Stephen is most impressed by this artist because he not only shares his own enthusiasm for buildings, but owns this green Ford Galaxy, conveniently parked beside the Smithsonian. Stephen immediately decides to draw the car while he and the mason discuss the merits and aesthetic superiority of great classic cars they have known. When he has finished the drawing, Stephen insists on being taken to the Cathedral (which is not part of the morning's agenda) because the mason is now a hero and his suggestion must be obeyed.

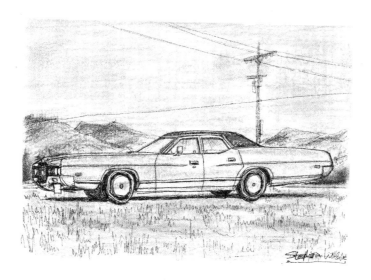

THE CATHEDRAL OF SS PETER AND PAUL

This remarkable Gothic cathedral, which was begun in 1907 and finally completed in 1990, is gloriously situated out of the centre of Washington and is approached by driving up what Stephen calls 'Embassy Row' because all the embassies are located in this area of the city. Stephen draws the west front of the cathedral from a park bench on the lawn in front of the building.

We walk over to see the Bishop's garden and, going through a romanesque arch, find ourselves in a small, secret maze of grottoes, topiary and an enchantingly picturesque herb garden. Stephen sketches the garden but is distracted by an animated dialogue between the gardener and two American tourists on the contents of their own herb garden. Stephen grabs another pad of drawing paper and hastily caricatures these two American super-fatties. The humorous aspect of Stephen's mind can never be under-estimated and it is this attractive quality which makes him such an enjoyable travelling companion.

The human comedy is never far from his perception of the world. His visual and mental grasp of a complex visual field together with his capacity to depict it is integrally linked to his ability to produce caricatures. He instantly recognises the characteristic features which define the individuality of a given face and his ludic sense skilfully communicates this with an economy of line which is both masterly and sententious.

THE JEFFERSON MEMORIAL

We are determined to defeat the 105°F temperature and accompanying humidity by starting work very early in the morning while it is still possible for Stephen to work in comfort. We seat ourselves opposite the Jefferson Memorial on the other side of the Potomac River. Nobody is about save a lone fisherman who is having a picnic breakfast. He has just caught a perch with his roach pole and also has a more sophisticated rod (complete with bell) for hooking catfish. The bell rings if a catfish has attached itself to the bait. Meanwhile, the fisherman sits on one of the wooden park benches eating his sandwiches and awaiting the sound of music.

Stephen is not interested in fishing – although we once spent an afternoon teaching him to cast but he very smartly removed himself from 'the filthy worms' and the endless untying of tangled tackle, saying, 'I'll just go and draw the river instead'. Annette proved a much better fisherman than her brother.

The Jefferson Memorial, built in 1943, is another neo-classical monument, adapted, very loosely, from the Pantheon in Rome. Stephen sketches in pencil and decides to colour the drawing later. It is completed in London on our return. The drawing has a secular imperial feeling and the domed rotunda has an almost tangible quality, smooth like the shell of an egg. It rises starkly against a cloudless sky, dramatised by Stephen's use of the blank paper as colour in itself.

Stephen Wiltshire

THE WILLARD HOTEL

We have tea at the Willard Hotel because the humidity in Washington in July is such that drawing outside in the afternoon is a penance. Stephen, well fortified by coke and crisps, pencils the interior lobby of the hotel as we talk. This turn-of-the-century *beaux arts* interior has recently been renovated. Grand American hotels eschew minimalism in favour of ornate marbled effects, gold-leaf ornamentation, serious stucco moulding, and immensely comfortable sofas and chairs. They exude material wealth and comfort and the standard of service is uniformly high.

Stephen responds well to intricate detail and decides to complete the drawing in pen while we are there. Frequently drawings are sketched in pencil to be completed later, but he is enjoying himself and has no desire to leave the air-conditioned comfort of this hotel. How right! The drawing takes one and a half hours to complete and Stephen prolongs his departure by suggesting a quick sketch of Andrew who is reading a newspaper beside us. This authentic portrait arises from Stephen's recognition of the particular asymmetry of each individual's face. He does not stray from the anatomical structure but registers the impression made on him by the face which has its own characteristic rhythm, and it is this ineffable rhythm which creates the likeness.

UNION STATION

Union Station has a most beautiful, grandiose interior structure originally designed by the eminent architect, Daniel Burnham, in 1908 but the decline of rail travel in the course of this century led to dilapidation and decay. Fortunately, Burnham's original design has been reincarnated at vast expense within the last few years and the result is a resounding triumph. It must stand as one of the great railway stations of the world.

Stephen, Andrew and I have lunch at the central café the day prior to the execution of this drawing. We are simply here to have a look at the interior and gauge Stephen's response. He is thrilled by the structure and we decide to return the following day to draw. At the other end of the station, Stephen spots a fat gentleman who has just plonked himself down, rather breathlessly, on a central banquette which Stephen insists on sketching before we leave.

The following day, we return to draw the interior. Chairs (shown stacked in the central area because it is still early) are borrowed from the restaurant manager so that Stephen can improvise an easel. He sits at the far end of the station, sketching in pencil. The idea is to capture the spatial dynamics of this magnificent 96-foot high barrel-vaulted ceiling and to illustrate the detailed craftsmanship both on the ceiling and in the arched recesses on the right. The drawing is completed later in pen, from memory with the pencil sketch to guide him. It is a masterly drawing which conveys the space and depth while illustrating the beauty of this interior.

SAN FRANCISCO

Our second trip takes place in November 1991. It is the start of a major expedition which will embrace San Francisco, Los Angeles and Arizona.

For Stephen, San Francisco is a dance to the music of time: earthquake paradise, cable-car carnival, Transamerica Pyramid and a car spied downtown in this glorious city with the registration number 'AUTISM 2'. Our autistic hero has found Nirvana on the West Coast. Dr Oliver Sacks joins our party in this city together with the ABC 20/20 crew who are making a television documentary on Stephen.

VIEW FROM THE FOUR SEASONS CLIFT HOTEL

Stephen, Andrew and I arrive in San Francisco and Jeff Knollmiller of Knollmiller Communications has kindly arranged accommodation for our party at this delightful hotel. The hotel management provides Stephen with a spectacular view from his bedroom window which is rapturously greeted by our artist. Such thoughtfulness on the part of the hotel is hugely appreciated because Stephen is most responsive to what he terms 'the grand view'. He instantly recognises the Bay Bridge in the background, part of which had collapsed during the earthquake in 1989. Earthquakes are his passion. The television is not switched on (is Stephen ill?) but, without bothering to unpack, he helps himself to a coke, takes a chair and seats himself at the window to draw the view. ABS 20/20 film Stephen drawing this view in pen the following day.

Andrew and I unpack in our room which interconnects with that of Stephen's. We are both studiously ignored since he has withdrawn completely into his own world to draw. I glance round the door periodically to see him taking photographs of the view and then returning to the drawing, humming like a wasp and occasionally jumping up frantically when he hears an ambulance or police siren. He is inordinately fond of the noise of sirens which he can simulate to perfection and there's no shortage of this orchestral accompaniment in American cities.

St Paulus Lutheran Church

On our first morning in this beautiful city, Stephen, Andrew and I take the sketch-pads and go for a walk around the streets to get a feel for what most Americans will tell you is 'the most European of cities'. The epithet is not correct. San Francisco exemplifies Old America and although it may appear 'European' to Americans by contrast to other US cities, it sings Old America to European eyes.

It is a coincidence, therefore, that our walk leads to this church in Eddy Street; it is conveniently situated opposite a derelict house and garden, ideal for setting up Stephen's travelling-stool in the overgrown garden and just out of the glare of the sun.

I tell Stephen that it was built in the late nineteenth century and is loosely based on Chartres Cathedral. Stephen laughs and says, 'it's kind of Gothic,' and then adds, 'it's not Notre Dame!'

We are joined in the garden by various social marginals who all admire Stephen's drawing, commend him to the Almighty and stumble off, clutching their bottles of half-consumed liquor which Stephen is offered but declines.

THE ISLAMIC THEATER GARAGE

Our walk takes us to Geary Street and is interrupted by Stephen who sees a 1954 Cadillac disappearing into the bowels of this Islamic structure. Unable to draw the vanished vehicle, he sketches the building instead: a grander garage façade would be hard to find.

Originally built as the local Shriners' Islamic Temple in 1917, it subsequently became the Alcazar Theater, and is now a garage on the ground floor while the upper part is being restored – although we fail to find out what eventually it will serve. All the characteristic features of the building are Islamic: and Stephen, who loves elaborate façades of a highly intricate nature, is well pleased with his 'find' because it provides compulsive viewing on two fronts: an endless stream of vanishing Cadillacs into the garage, and an attractive building to draw which he colours on his return to the hotel.

SAN FRANCISCO OPERA HOUSE

The ABC 20/20 team take Stephen on a tour of San Francisco and film Stephen while he sits in front of the Opera House, sketching the building and reciting the names of the passing cars. The drawing is a very good example of Stephen's freehand style.

When the drawing is finished, Stephen chooses his lunchtime menu and the crew take us to a drive-in hamburger parlour which celebrates 1950s' nostalgia. These places are acquired tastes which I find appalling and Stephen adores. The cartoon of the crew, however, is a different matter. This is drawn after the hamburger bonanza. An epicene Andrew, seated on the left of the drawing, suggests that this drawing represents 'Gorbachev's henchmen'. The 20/20 producer, Joe Pfifferling, third from the right, appears lachrymose but the photographer, Donna Morrison, is given a smile of beatific composure (Stephen likes blonde-haired girls) while Bob Brown, the writer and presenter of the programme, appears to epitomise the spirit of eternal youth.

THREE VIEWS OF THE GOLDEN GATE BRIDGE

As its name would not suggest, the Golden Gate is painted an unmistakable red. The bridge is a glowing testament to suspension technology. Initially, the idea of constructing a bridge to connect the mile-stretch between San Francisco and Marin County was dismissed by the prophets of doom as a lunatic enterprise. The incredible power of the tides in the bay and the depth of the water appeared to legislate against any such technology overcoming these obstacles. Modern technology triumphed, however, and the Golden Gate is now San Francisco's most memorable landmark.

The ABC 20/20 crew drive us to the bridge which Stephen draws from various angles. The first drawing is the most visually dramatic and is chosen by the cameraman, Terry Morrison, for precisely these reasons. (Although Stephen has filmed with TV crews all over the world, it is the first time we have a cameraman whose mind is not replete with visual clichés). This view is spectacular and has to be drawn quickly today because the mist and cloud acts like a theatrical curtain, a 'now you see it, now you don't' experience.

Andrew wanders off to watch the pelicans flying overhead and reports back to announce that there are eider duck swimming in the bay far below where he is standing on the cliff tops. As ornithological expert, I have no reason to doubt his sightings until Terry Morrison states that in fact they are human surfers. This fits well with the distorted view of the bridge that Stephen is drawing. So much depends upon prior knowledge. Vision alone is not sufficient. Few would guess that Stephen's drawing illustrates the Golden Gate from this angle. In the context of all three drawings, however, the bridge is easy to understand. The second sketch is drawn from Marin County, as is the final drawing. Stephen uses a larger pad for the third drawing which he is unable to balance on his arm. I act as easel and he props the pad on my back as I bend over. Such is the submissive role of the European woman . . . The sketch takes ten minutes to complete. Few artists could use a pen so sparingly to suggest so much.

CHINATOWN

This is Chinatown's Grant Avenue, seen here looking south towards the city's central shopping district. America's largest Chinese quarter spreads itself over twenty-four square blocks of downtown San Francisco.

The Chinese symbols give little problem to Stephen. His visual apprehension is such that they present themselves as patterns. Their meaning does not interest him. His internal visual lexicon masters all foreign signs instantly (as seen in the Tokyo sketch in the introduction) and was first noted in the drawing of the GUM department store in Moscow (illustrated in *Floating Cities*).

No one has drawn parked cars with such enthusiasm and obvious delight. Stephen's unerring eye has grasped the character of Chinatown and he has given it his full attention.

PACIFIC HEIGHTS

Oliver Sacks has hired a car and, like Toad of Toad Hall, with whom he has much in common, wishes to 'go motoring'. He drives Stephen, Andrew and myself to Pacific Heights which is San Francisco's ghetto for the super-rich. We start by showing Stephen the city's steepest hill – so steep in fact that only pedestrians (joggers today) can use the uppermost windy stretch where vehicles are prohibited.

Stephen produces a quick sketch of the view as we enjoy the spectacle of a street happening which must be a rather unusual event in this rarefied atmosphere of conspicuous affluence. A man has just run naked down the street to the consternation of a lady who has chosen to espy him from the top floor of her house. We, unfortunately, miss the naked man but cannot miss her or the outraged neighbours. Stephen turns up the volume of his Walkman and ignores them all.

On completion of the little sketch which well illustrates the desirability of this neighbourhood because the views are magnificent, we walk around the area in search of architectural splendours. This Italianate palazzo (opposite) is chosen for its Edgar Allan Poe qualities of stygian gloom. Oliver wants to know who lives here and bravely asks a passer-by (the *only* passer-by as people from Pacific Heights don't walk if they can ride) and is met with one of life's better ripostes: 'I don't know *who* lives there but *something's* lived there for years.'

Stephen W.

As Stephen props his pad on a parked car to draw, Oliver stands at a distance, scribbling in his notepad (which acts as his umbilical cord, connecting him to the universe through language) and snorting with laughter. I try to inveigle my way into the exotic houses built around interior courtyards. Numerous vans are unloading flower arrangements of stultifying proportions while container meals appear from caterers' vans as household staff wave directions. At one house, I am waved in with the boeuf bourguignone but quickly waved out again when I explain my real mission. Partying is paramount. One particular Venetian-style courtyard is breathtakingly beautiful and the owner, dressed in *le style anglais* (a style strictly for foreigners) consents to Stephen's presence for 'no more than ten minutes because we are partying tonight' but, by this time, I'm so exhausted by their Gatsby fantasies that I decide to keep to exteriors.

HYDE LINE CABLE CAR

This drawing is executed from a photograph provided by the US Travel and Tourism Administration. The Hyde Street Line depicted here is the most spectacular in terms of loops and swoops which make it San Francisco's most enjoyable ride. Alcatraz can be seen in the distance.

Stephen chose this photograph himself from a selection which we were given, and laboured over this drawing for several hours. He found the image immensely appealing and it is surely in part the inspiration for Quintessential San Francisco on page 87.

PALACE OF FINE ARTS

This was built for the city's Panama–Pacific Exposition in 1915. Stephen's three drawings, taken from photographs, illustrate the Palace and the lagoon, the peristyle and the rotunda.

The structure was never conceived as having a life beyond that of the Exposition, but such was the success of this Roman folly that models eventually replaced the original structure and today it stands as one of the key features of the city. It represents both 'the grandeur that was Rome' and a romantic nostalgia, created by carefully overgrown shrubs and trees which lend a *tristesse* to the complex. Paradoxically, the dilapidation and decay of this splendidly majestic ruin is, in fact, a hymn to twentieth-century fakery.

Stephen's three drawings do full justice to this anachronistic complex which serves to enhance this wonderful city.

THE CIRCLE GALLERY

Maiden Lane, which runs off Union Square, is a fashionable pedestrian precinct with an unmistakable whiff of arch-bohemian affluence. We are having lunch outside, positioned at a table which will provide the best view of Frank Lloyd Wright's façade which is now the Circle Gallery. This marvellous building was originally designed as a shop, the Helga Howie Boutique. Nothing so vulgar as window displays – the exterior façade is a brick wall and the only way in is a sublime, arched, cave-like entrance. Few buildings speak so eloquently of their masters but this gem could stand as Wright's signature tune. It is as strikingly original today as it must have appeared in 1948 when the store opened. Nothing else in this charming, tree-lined street compares with the creative genius of Wright's cube.

Stephen draws the view from the table where he sits which will illustrate the gallery in relation to the entire street. His roving eye is frequently drawn to the pretty fair-haired American girls who are window-shopping in Maiden Lane (no cars in this pedestrianised zone to compete with the females). The drawing is produced by remote hand control as Stephen's gaze follows a particularly glamorous blonde. His head does a 180° turn as his hand continues to sketch the street in front. When Andrew asks Stephen what he thinks of the building, he says, 'She's beautiful!'

QUINTESSENTIAL SAN FRANCISCO

One evening, just before the end of our stay in this vibrant city, Stephen is giving Andrew and me an art show of his San Francisco drawings in his bedroom at the Four Seasons Clift Hotel. I am sketched first, sitting on his bed before the show commences. He is very proud of his work and introduces each drawing with a brief description of the location, but then says, 'But I haven't got Union Square.' As we were crossing this square the previous day, Stephen stopped to ask us to take his photograph in front of the buildings. This was very unusual because, being extremely unvain, Stephen rarely has any desire to see himself in photographs. Immediately he mentions the absence of Union Square, I recall this curious event. 'Well, I like this square and I'll just draw it now,' he says. An instant sketch is produced, rubbed with a little colour and held up for inspection. Such freedom of line is bewitching.

Stephen feels that he has now completed San Francisco but I still think something is missing. I can't articulate what it is but suggest that it might be the *spirit* of the place. What we need is 'quintessential San Francisco' – that which most conjures up this beautiful city. Stephen is gazing at me in a concentrated but equally detached manner with a wonderful grin on his face as I struggle to convey to him these abstract feelings. Suddenly, he grabs his pen, sketches this exquisite vision, rubs in a bit of colour with his crayons and announces with a flourish, 'That's it!' and for me, this is 'it' – the most cherished drawing of them all because Stephen's imagination has caught the characteristic features in those inimitable whimsical lines.

LOS ANGELES

We leave the ABC 20/20 crew in San Francisco to head for Los Angeles. Two and a half days will be spent in this city and we leave Stephen to choose the itinerary because it is a virtual impossibility to cover downtown LA in such a short space of time. His selection comprises Hollywood, Hollywood Boulevard, Sunset Boulevard, Wilshire Boulevard (with which he identifies) and Santa Monica. It is a celebratory vision which reflects Stephen's interests and, as such, it is of particular fascination. Social problems, riots, political unease and urban decay are definitely not of interest to this teenager, who has an engaging ability to ignore what he does not like or understand. Los Angeles is celluloid fantasy to him and the dream must not be tarnished.

WILSHIRE BOULEVARD

Our arrival at the Regent Beverly Wilshire Hotel creates tidal ecstasy in Stephen. The view down Wilshire Boulevard, festooned with Christmas decorations, is drawn on our arrival as he sits in his room enjoying a hamburger/coke lunch, accompanied by myriad presents from the hotel management including a video of *Pretty Woman* which was filmed in and around the hotel. This small figure, seated in front of his favourite lunch, with coke in the ice bucket and orchids beside the French fries, grinning from ear to ear, is intoxicatingly delightful.

We go downstairs after lunch so we can have coffee in the lobby bar. It is full of ladies lunching lightly on angel hair pasta, champagne and chablis. The pianist plays 'Smoke Gets In Your Eyes' and Stephen immediately turns up the volume on his Walkman. A quick sketch is produced to entertain us before we all depart.

SET FOR THE FRESH PRINCE OF BEL AIR

Our old friend, Joe Marcell, plays the butler in this popular television series. He arranges for Stephen, Andrew and me to come to the studios in Hollywood so that Stephen may have the opportunity to draw one of the sets.

The sitting-room is chosen by our artist and he seats himself in the director's high chair. The drawing is unusual in that he chooses to include the overhead lighting which the television viewers will never see. This addition firmly established the factitious nature of the set and illustrates the quiet originality of Stephen's mind.

A portrait of Joe, who also comes from St Lucia like Stephen's mother, is produced over cokes on the adjoining set, that of the kitchen. Stephen loves American soaps and feels himself to be part of this series now that he's been given a conducted 'behind the scenes' tour. Joe should be canonised for making this possible because, for Stephen, Hollywood represents an integral part of his American dream.

MANN'S CHINESE THEATER

Stephen chooses Mann's Chinese Theater on this boulevard because it immortalises cinema kitsch. He stands on Elton John's celebratory paving stone to draw the theater, holding his pad at an impossible angle to avoid a collision with the seething cineasts. An Australian honeymoon couple, who have seen him on CBS 60 Minutes Australia, engage him in conversation which prompts a party of South Africans, who have seen him on BBC's QED programme, to join us. They are followed by Japanese, Dutch and Swedish tourists who also wish to congratulate Stephen. He smiles, raises his hand to the assembled crowd and says, 'Hi fans, good to see you!' This star idiom is picked up by Stephen from television and he proceeds to imitate it. It is far removed from a belief in his own stardom which is virtually non-existent. Stephen is extremely modest and self-effacing but to those who are present today, he is Hollywood's equal. Andrew and I then take it in turns to act as easel as Stephen props his drawing pad on our backs.

As we drive up Sunset Boulevard, Stephen is in his element sitting up front in the cab, his Walkman rattling in his ear, snapping cars with his yellow instamatic for the Great American Collection, the majority of which are the big gas-guzzlers of the 1960s, the larger the wheelbase, the better. Dirty, bashed specimens are ignored.

94

SUNSET BOULEVARD

Stephen's drawing of Sunset Boulevard is a classic: no buildings, no cars, no people – a distillation of urban California and is Stephen's most informed comment to date. It was entirely his idea to draw the street like this, and it took our breath away.

THE PIERHEAD, SANTA MONICA

This view is suggested to Stephen by Joe Pfifferling, the ABC producer, while we are filming in San Francisco. Stephen sits on a bench amongst the palm trees as our Iranian cab driver tells the park rangers about Stephen's incredible abilities. Retired couples bask in the sunshine, head-phoned joggers jiggle past, a total stranger gives me a lecture on crime in Los Angles which Stephen enjoys because he provides a chorus of his police siren noises to this frenzied monologue. Andrew escapes to buy films for Stephen's camera and I finally manage to slip drawing pad and pens to Stephen whilst continuing to listen to 'the Sodom and Gomorrah that is LA today'.

The colour drawing on the next page is a meditation on a seascape and displays acute sensitivity in the handling of its subject. It is unusual work in that it concerns absence and has never been attempted by Stephen before. He captures the serenity and the mood of contemplation.

One of the park rangers, who informs Stephen that the composer for the theme music in *Rain Man* runs here every day, is joined by a friend who wants to see Stephen work. The small sketch on this page is quickly drawn to prove how easy it is and Stephen holds it up after four minutes, saying, 'There!' He is obviously hoping to meet the *Rain Man* composer and so is reluctant to leave his perch on the park bench in case the wonder man arrives. To delay departure, he suggests drawing the palm trees, overleaf. The composer fails to materialise.

Stephen consoles himself by singing the entire score of *Rain Man* from memory as we drive further along the coast to Marina del Rey to lunch at Shanghai Red's, a magical restaurant suggested to us by the mystery writer, Joe Hansen, who joins our little party for lunch. En route, we pass a restaurant with the unfortunate name of 'The Pelican's Catch'. We tell Stephen that pelicans regurgitate their food: as he hates fish, he thinks this is eminently sensible.

Stephen sketches the view from the restaurant at Shanghai Red's as we sit in the midday sun with our drinks. Marina del Rey is the world's largest man-made small-boat harbour.

Stephen Wiltshire

MEMORIES OF THE WEST COAST

Two months after our trip to the West Coast, Stephen produces this memory drawing of his favourite views. These unsolicited pen drawings illustrate his abiding interest in 'Americana' and highlight his passion for travel. Visual images serve to stimulate and nurture his development. He selects and distils the memories he has retained from his trips which he then commits to paper. It is our entrance to his world and a deeply felt form of communication for Stephen.

The drawing is a pot-pourri of San Francisco, Santa Monica, Beverly Hills and Los Angeles – a charming montage of the lived experience of this journey.

ARIZONA

While we were filming in London with CBS 60 Minutes Australia in the spring of 1991, Jeff McMullin, the programme's presenter, suggested we include a visit to the Canyon de Chelly in Stephen's next book. His enthusiasm was considerable but we had no contacts in Arizona. The possibility seemed delightful but remote in the extreme. Then, on a Sunday morning shortly after the completion of the Australian film, Stephen, Annette, Andrew and I were sitting beneath Canning's statue in Parliament Square fulfilling a commission for the Securities and Investment Board when a party of four American girls stopped to watch Stephen draw. They were overheard to speak of Phoenix, Arizona, and so we introduced ourselves to one of the party, Nicole Olton, president of Edswest Event and Destination Services in Arizona. Nicole listened, and there and then agreed to make all the arrangements and organise sponsorship for a visit to Arizona in November. Without this miraculous encounter with 'the desert saint', this section of the book could not have been realised.

We have arranged to rejoin Oliver Sacks in Las Vegas where we collect a 1991 Lincoln Continental so Oliver, Stephen, Andrew and I can drive to Phoenix. Stephen would have preferred a 1972 Chevrolet Impala but the hire company cannot produce a car older than 1990.

    It is a warm and beautiful day and we do not anticipate any hitches during the five-hour cross-country drive. None of us is aware that there is an hour's time difference between Nevada and Phoenix, Arizona, but after we cross the state line at the Hoover Dam a highway clock shows not 12.30 but 1.30 pm and it begins to sink in that we are going to be late for the reception that evening at the Lovena Ohl Gallery in Scottsdale. Then, on the freeway, we suddenly find ourselves in a long south-bound tail-back of cars and trucks which stretches as far as the eye can see. We learn there's a natural gas leak which has closed the turn off ahead to Flagstaff. Only traffic to Phoenix is allowed through but it takes an hour to inch our way to the road block. Oliver lacks Stephen's Eastern-style acceptance of interminable delays and removes himself from the car to stroll beside us in the scrub of the central reservation – a modern-day Christ in the Wilderness – which Stephen is quick to capture.

THE GRAND CANYON

We motor southwards through a cactus landscape orchestrated by a spectacular sunset, gratefully reaching Scottsdale, but an hour and a half later than we intend. The reception has been arranged for Stephen by kind hosts, Lovena Ohl and Bill Faust whose warm welcome dissolves our embarrassment. Stephen gives an eloquent impromptu performance for the guests describing all the drawings he has completed on this leg of the trip.

We spend the night at the Scottsdale Princess Resort – a fabulous Moorish-style palace modelled on the Palais Salaam in Taroudant, in Morocco. The following morning, we set off with Nicole and her driver and guide Warren Fisher on a three-day journey that will end at the Canyon de Chelly. En route to Flagstaff, we stop at intervals to see Montezuma's castle, Bell Rock, and photograph dramatic views of the San Francisco peaks. We witness sunset over the Grand Canyon and spend the first night at the Grand Canyon National Park Lodge as guests of Joyce Vaughan.

Stephen is enthralled by a landscape which is so visually arresting and which is quite foreign to him. He is mesmerised by the dramatic light changes over the Grand Canyon which alter the evening view from a sharp outline to a soft focus purple haze within a matter of minutes as we watch, bewitched. We abandon all thoughts of drawing because it seems of far greater importance to leave Stephen to absorb the scenery and seize the opportunity to provide him with a unique visual landscape which he would, or would not, be able to recreate at his leisure on our return to England.

The following morning, we are taken on a helicopter ride over the canyon from the south to the north rim. The canyon has a new set of colours to display as the strong morning light has totally altered this wonderland of illusions. Papillon Grand Canyon Helicopters provide this ride for Stephen, who is seated beside the pilot in a state of private ecstasy, with Andrew, Oliver Sacks and myself in the rear.

The colour illustrations which follow were all produced on Stephen's return to London. It took four weeks of trial and error before Stephen acquired a technique which would enable him to use colour, not as an additive but as a means of conveying space, depth and atmosphere. The triumphant success of this venture was not assured when he started. For an artist who has always excelled as a draughtsman and not as a colourist, this challenge was colossal. To assist him, Stephen used photographs, sketches which he had pencilled while he was in Arizona and, best of all, his visual memory of this unique landscape.

Stephen Wiltshire

HOPILAND

Our final day is spent in Hopiland where Verma and Robert Rhodes act as our guides. It is at their house, not far from Hotevilla on the Hopi reservation that we all have lunch before setting off to Old Oraibi, the oldest continuously inhabited town in the United States (since AD 1150) where Stephen executes this memory drawing of a Mennonite Church (opposite) which ominously shadows the village of Oraibi. We are informed that it had been struck by lightning twice which explains its ruined state today. Alternatively, one might more credibly adhere to the view that it was destroyed by the Hopis who resented the philistine, moralising presence of these evangelical fanatics. While Hopi dances were being performed in the plaza, the Mennonites would march their choir, accompanied by a harmonium, to the dance plaza in order to drown out the infidel. Nineteenth-century belief was such that the Indians would be 'civilised' by stripping them of their own culture.

On leaving Old Oraibi, we head for Walpi, an ancient village on first mesa. Perched on cliff-tops, it commands a superlative view of the surrounding desert. We are not permitted to take photographs nor is drawing allowed. The Hopi feel, with considerable justification, that they have been subjected to the intrusive presence of anthropologists and other visitors throughout the years and are no longer prepared to present themselves as exhibits or case studies to outsiders. The village – archaeologists suggest Walpi is at least eight hundred years old – is a fascinating social document of Indian life as seen through its buildings, its people and its arts and crafts, but it is impossible not to feel voyeuristic.

The Hopi emerge from their houses with pottery or kachina dolls for sale. The latter are as light as thread, carved from the roots of the cottonwood tree; it feels like balsa wood. The village children are playing a version of American football and two tiny children sit cross-legged in the sand playing cards.

Our guide, Robert Rhodes, shows us the village plaza where formerly the famous Snake Dance was performed in which Hopi priests carried rattlesnakes and other serpents – some of them in their mouths. The snakes, which live underground, are seen as the natural intercessors to the gods who, in Hopi theology, inhabit the underworld. This particular ritual has now been abandoned at Walpi because the present generation is no longer able to perfect the dance. The Hopi would rather abandon their traditional dance than have it incorrectly interpreted. Andrew wonders if these people will continue to live 'hopily ever after' as their culture declines.

Stephen draws the village from memory after we leave (opposite). The sketch below illustrates a 1975 Chevrolet Impala mounted on blocks, in pristine condition. Such is Stephen's euphoria at finding this beat-up car in the village that the glorious wreck has become lovingly re-created as a contender for the Arizona Highways. Card-players are seated to the right and a football match can be seen in the background.

THE CANYON DE CHELLY

We spend the night at a motel beside the Canyon de Chelly in order to set off early into the canyon the following day. We are still in north-eastern Arizona but no longer on the Hopi reservation but in the heart of the Navajo nation. The original inhabitants of the canyon were the Anasazi until their mysterious disappearance in AD 1300 (possibly caused by drought). The Hopi subsequently took up occupation until 1700 when they were replaced by the Navajo.

Our genial Navajo guide, Justin Tso, gives us a conducted tour of the canyon in his specially fitted camper van. Only the foolhardy would drive into this labyrinthine canyon without a guide because it is all too easy for vehicles to sink into the wet sands of the canyon floor. Indeed, within minutes of entering the canyon, we pass a vehicle that has met this ignominious end. It would be hard to find a more interesting Navajo guide and mentor than Justin who summons up the ancestral voices of his tribe including that of his great grandmother, one of the few who survived the Long Walk in 1864 when the Navajo were forced to surrender to Kit Carson in the Canyon de Chelly and to walk to their place of exile, the reservation at Fort Sumner in New Mexico.

The red sandstone canyon is awe-inspiring in its majesty. Sheer walls, dramatically eroded formations and a network of deeply sculpted sandstone passages reveal occupation from the early years of the Christian era. It commands an authority and quasi-spiritual presence which is unrivalled in the state of Arizona.

We return to spend our last night at the Scottsdale Princess Resort. The following morning, Warren Fisher and Nicole collect us to drive to Taliesin West, the Frank Lloyd Wright Foundation from which the maverick messiah has long since departed. We are given a conducted tour of this prairie residence which Stephen sketches before we depart for the airport and the long journey back to London.

NEW YORK

This is our final trip to complete The American Dream. New York is 'the city of cities' to Stephen, a secular temple of all his passions: the Empire State Building, Twin Trade Towers, Chrysler Building, yellow cabs, police sirens, fire-engines and ambulances whooping their distinctive registers, hamburgers and pretty girls and the chance to bounce down Fifth Avenue feeling ten feet tall because you are going to see your own exhibition of the *Floating Cities* drawings exhibited in the heart of Manhattan.

THE PIERRE HOTEL

The Pierre Hotel provides Stephen with a suite on the top floor which commands a superlative view over Central Park. It is a private paradise for him and the success of his New York trip is due in no small part to the kindness of the manager, Herbert Pliessnig, who devotes considerable attention to our artist.

We request a photograph of the hotel prior to our visit to familiarise Stephen with his forthcoming environment. I leave the picture at Stephen's house and he, unrequested, brings this drawing to show me the following week. By capturing the hotel on paper, the trip becomes a reality in his mind. Stephen needs to visualise his surroundings because a detailed verbal explanation is difficult to comprehend.

On our arrival in New York late one night at the end of January 1992, he spies the hotel from the taxi although it is several blocks away. The taxi driver is duly informed by Stephen: 'That's our hotel over there, The Pierre. Best view of Central Park.'

St Paul's Chapel and Churchyard

This is our first morning in New York City. Stephen, Annette, my colleague Liz Fairbairn and I decide to go to St Paul's to draw as it is the oldest church in the city.

Our cab driver doesn't speak English, has no idea where the church is and confirms what I've always suspected about some New York cabbies: they have an intelligence less than plant life and if they do speak English (which is rare) it's only in the imperative mode. All such assumptions are quickly overturned when we arrive finally at our destination and walk round the building trying to find an angle out of the wind from which to draw. A man jumps out of a cab and rushes over to us to say, 'I've just left my cab running in the middle of the street because I want to congratulate Stephen on his appearance on 20/20.' He proceeds to talk with considerable knowledge about autism and I immediately decide to hire him for the day. He's the most unusual New York cabbie I'd ever met: sane, knowledgeable and perfectly charming. This proposal is greeted with much laughter as he reveals that he's the passenger, not the cab-driver. 'Actually, I'm the saxophonist for David Bowie and Duran Duran.'

Stephen sketches the church as he sits on his travelling-stool outside a deli as the waiters inside beckon him to come and join them. They have also seen the TV programme; curiously they do not wish to watch him draw but would love to shake his hand.

As it is Sunday, we assume that there will be a service in the church. This is not the case but the church provides a different kind of service – shelter for the homeless who are all fast asleep in the pews. One bearded social marginal is awake, reading a battered paperback copy of *The American Dream*. Is this a portent of the chance encounter with Norman Mailer in Brooklyn Heights three days later? We tiptoe round the nave in order not to disturb their slumbers and decide that we cannot draw this lovely eighteenth-century interior because it seems an invasion of their privacy. I buy two postcards instead and we creep out. The interior is drawn from the photograph (no vagrants in evidence!) as is the view of the church from Broadway which illustrates the added triangular pedimented portico. This is the east end of the church (the first drawing shows the church from the west front) because when Broadway became an important thoroughfare, New Yorkers wanted a suitably impressive façade to face the street.

ST PATRICK'S CATHEDRAL

Stephen, Liz (below), a journalist and I go to St Patrick's Cathedral the next morning. Stephen sits on his stool beside Liz sketching this neo-gothic edifice which was built in the late nineteenth century. Passers-by, who have marvelled at Stephen's talent as shown on the ABC 20/20 documentary a few days previously, come up to congratulate him and chat. Stephen beams and says 'Hi!' as he continues to draw, and chats to them merrily.

This is a particularly fascinating drawing because the rigidity of the actual stone carving has been transformed by Stephen's fluid line to create the impression of a decorated thirteenth-century Gothic style which is far more appealing.

I show it to Norman Mailer later in the week who does not instantly recognise it as St Patrick's but thinks it has much more in common with the great French cathedrals. Such is the illusory nature of art!

CITY HALL

We walk round the corner from St Paul's to City Hall (1802-11), which will be our second drawing of the morning. The sketching itinerary is such that Stephen and I try to choose buildings which are all within walking distance of the particular area in which we find ourselves.

   This drawing is produced from the park in front of the building and illustrates the elegant French influence of this downtown façade.

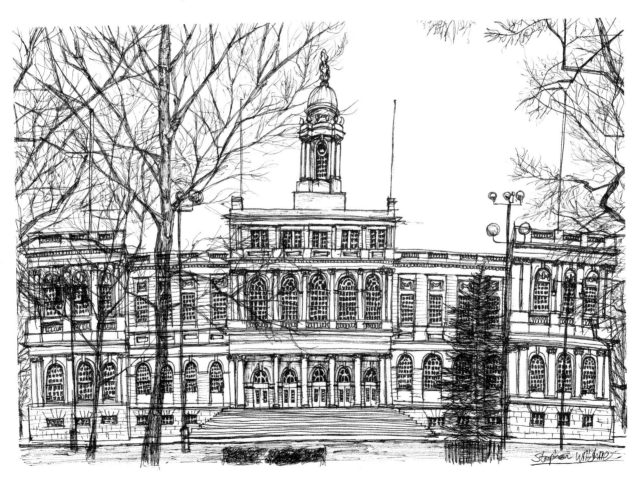

METROPOLITAN OPERA HOUSE

Stephen is seated in front of the building to sketch this drawing straight into pen. The fountain in the foreground is evoked by using the paper itself to suggest transparency, Stephen choosing to outline the contours of the water only. The two end windows give a glimpse of the Chagalls which Stephen had registered although few artists would have considered the inclusion of their reflection in an exterior sketch.

The security guard for this building complex watches as Stephen works, informing us that the people are going to a performance of *Tanburger* – alas, not a hamburger that Stephen has ever tasted.

AERIAL VIEW OF THE FINANCIAL DISTRICT

This wonderful drawing is produced from a photograph lent to us by The United States Travel and Tourism Administration. Stephen chooses this particular image from a selection which he is given because he is magnetically drawn to aerial views which depict skyscrapers. For him, New York is defined by the energy created by the dense verticality of these architectural splendours. The civility of the brownstones on the Upper East Side lack the pulsating dynamism of Wall Street's thrusting vigour. His attitude is unequivocally of the present day and his Messianic urban vision celebrates clean, soaring, linear configurations.

The infinite patience which is devoted to this drawing is a measure of his unassuageable thirst for modernity.

Stephen Wiltshire.

TWIN TRADE TOWERS

Stephen is showing me his car drawings in the hotel bedroom when I glimpse this unusual sketch in his private collection. He tells me it is drawn from memory – four years after his first visit to New York with ITN News.

This singular drawing is notable for its quasi-abstract quality which one does not generally associate with Stephen's work. The towers soar obliquely, pitched against infinity. The sketch hovers delicately between representation and abstraction: further evidence that he possesses a creative imagination and proof that he does not simply draw what he sees.

COURTYARD OF THE FRICK MUSEUM

It is too cold to work outside this afternoon, so we all go to the Frick. Stephen draws the interior courtyard to illustrate the charm of this lovely museum. It is a delightful setting which calls for afternoon tea and a small orchestra. The stone benches are for serious aesthetes, however, and our sybaritic tendencies long for comfortable chairs while Stephen pens this exquisite freehand drawing with a speed which defies belief.

BROOKLYN HEIGHTS

Our trip to Brooklyn Heights is suggested by the ABC News Programme who have attended Stephen's opening of the *Floating Cities* exhibition in Manhattan and now wish to film him drawing in New York. They will feature Stephen on the News that same evening.

It is bitterly cold with an icy wind blowing in our faces – hardly conducive to sketching, or anything else. It is at these moments that we celebrate Stephen's astonishing speed in rendering lines on paper that miraculously cohere to produce this completed drawing.

We adjourn finally to the Promenade Restaurant in Brooklyn Heights for lunch. A familiar figure shuffles in who I think is Norman Mailer; the mischievous, twinkly blue eyes do not belong to any other face. I introduce myself to show him Stephen's drawings and he agrees to sign the Brooklyn Heights sketch. Stephen meets the author briefly and afterwards I tell him that Mailer is part of the fabric of New York and a superstar (not in the league of *Beverly Hills 90210* as far as Stephen is concerned, of course) whose novel title we shall share.

Norman Mailer

Washington Square North

This view is drawn from the park benches in Washington Square. I want Stephen to understand the architectural development of New York and to illustrate to him the former dignity and gentility of this neighbourhood as reflected in these houses. As far as Stephen is concerned, this is *not* New York and certainly not the reason why he so adores it. 'Now there's Times Square. I want to go to Times Square.' The tranquillity of this square is not to his taste but it does serve to give Stephen some sense of historical perspective.

The drawing is penned effortlessly as we talk of his dream location: a penthouse in New York where he will live as Artist in Residence.

In the evening, our extravagantly enthusiastic friends, Bobby Geisler and John Roberdeau, who have been long-time members of Stephen's fan club, hire a stretch limo for a night-time cruise with our artist around Manhattan. While we sail down Fifth Avenue, Stephen twiddles the dials beside his seat to illuminate the interior fairy lights, turns up the stereo and opens the drinks cabinet. The fairy lights twinkle intermittently at this grinning face who has reached the apogee of pleasure in the city of his dreams, surrounded by the vertical splendour of Manhattan's triumphantly modernist architecture. A can of iced Coke to hand, he peers through the windows of the limo, admiring the cherished urban nightscene of the greatest city in the world – New York.

VIEW FROM THE TOP OF THE EMPIRE STATE BUILDING

Stephen's favourite building in the whole of New York is the Empire State Building. It is the quintessential skyscraper and characterises what constitutes essential New York. He frequently draws it from memory and from photographs. The drawing on the left is drawn on the United Airlines flight on our way to New York. It is taken from an illustration in a magazine that Stephen finds on the plane. Stephen tells me that it was built in 1931 and I trade this piece of information by informing him that it used to be known as the Empty State Building during the 1930s slump. We discuss the case of Irma Eberhardt who achieved immortality by becoming the first successful suicide to leap from the top in 1933, the year in which King Kong made his spectacular ascent.

The Empire State Building generously agreed to exhibit Stephen's *Floating Cities* drawings in their Fifth Avenue Gallery. The memory drawing on the right was produced for the poster prior to our visit.

Stephen Tole, the Vice President of the ESB, and Lydia Ruth, the gallery manager, arrange for Stephen, Annette and me to be given a guided tour of the view from the observatory on the 102nd floor. The intention is that Stephen will sketch the view but the wind is icy and, unlike Stephen, I am incapable of spending more than two seconds in the open air at the top of this building. Stephen, ever obliging, says, 'Well, that's fine, I'll just do a memory drawing of the view later,' and the drawing on the next spread is what is produced that evening back at the hotel.

His ability to grasp a complex visual field and illustrate it graphically is well illustrated in this drawing. The Flatiron building, which fills the triangle where Fifth Avenue joins Broadway, carries the eye to the Twin Trade Towers. Stephen looked at the view for less than a minute. The Flatiron building is also drawn independently, and appears on the next spread also.

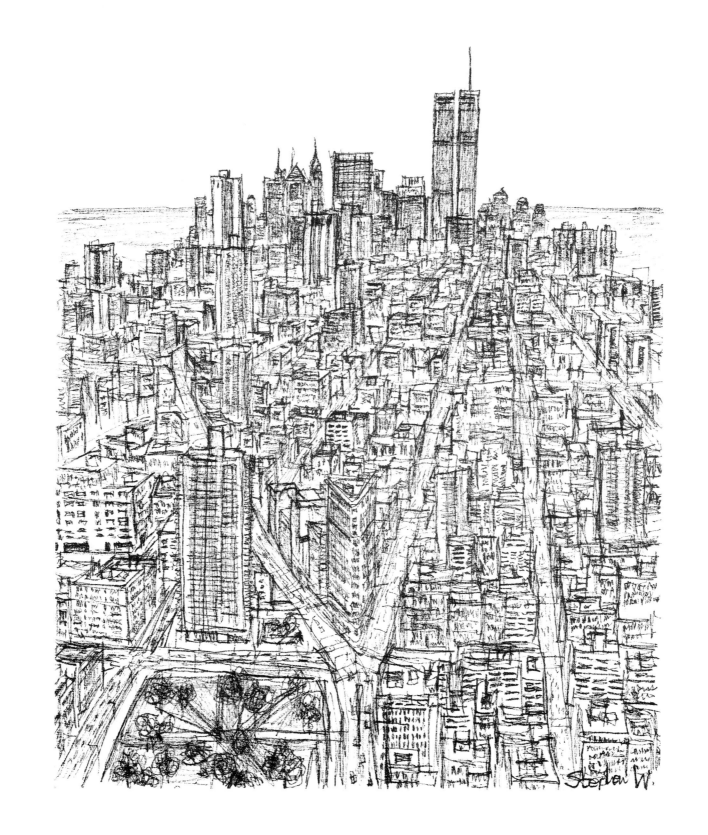

Aerial View of the Chrysler Building

Stephen is frustrated because I cannot find a close-up view of the Chrysler Building. A friend, Sarah Uffelman, is given the problem and promptly arranges a visit to the offices on the top of the Pan-Am Building belonging to Clay Finlay Inc. The view from these premises is such that the Chrysler spire is within conversational range. Stephen is delighted and Francis Finlay is most welcoming.

In 1930, the Chrysler exceeded the world's tallest structure at the time, the Eiffel Tower, by 64 feet. The tower rises to a shining stainless steel spire above concentric arches pierced by triangular windows. Stephen sits in the window of Clay Finlay's offices and sketches the top of the tower and the spire together with the view as it recedes into the far distance. On completion of the drawing, Stephen walks round the offices to scrutinise the view in the opposite direction – that of the Queensboro Bridge. We are unable to prolong our visit because Stephen is required to give an interview. The second sketch is produced over lunch as a memory drawing.

THE CHRYSLER BUILDING FROM MADISON & 46th STREET

The day after our visit to the offices of Clay Finlay Inc, Stephen, Liz and I are walking down Madison Avenue when Liz spots this view of the Chrysler building from the street. We explain to Stephen that Walter Chrysler wanted a building that would express both the luxury and the mechanical precision of that automobile in its jazz incarnations. Stephen sketches in the rain, protecting his sketch-pad by sitting on his travelling-stool underneath some convenient scaffolding. The building on the left is the upper façade of Grand Central Station.

GRAND CENTRAL STATION

Stephen sits in the middle of the station to draw this interior. He is immediately besieged by commuters who have seen him on television and they engage him in a barrage of questions which elicit Stephenesque responses:

'How did you learn perspective, Stephen?'

'I got it.'

'Have you ever considered training as an artist?'

'I'm an artist.'

'Do you like our Central Station?'

'I like the Chrysler Building.'

Everyone requests a drawing but Stephen simply smiles – that is, until a girl asks for a drawing of a Buick for her boyfriend. The station drawing is cast aside immediately and a meticulous memory sketch is produced of the car. A dedication is added, on instruction, and the finished work is handed over with a flourish and a big smile.

On returning to his original drawing, the crowd, having watched the car request being met, deluge Stephen with myriad suggestions. We cannot cope with their demands and Stephen bravely looks up at me and says, 'I think I'll draw this interior from my memory.' It's an elegant escape and so we pack our bags and leave the crowd, who wave him goodbye.

Too many voices simultaneously confuse Stephen but he will listen and concentrate on the voice which identifies his own predilections and respond accordingly.

PARK AVENUE

After we escape from Grand Central Station, Stephen asks to be taken via Park Avenue so he can look at the view down to the Pan-Am Building. This sketch is drawn as he leans against a lamp-post exchanging greetings with passing car drivers who have seen him on ABC 20/20. The drawing (opposite) is completed later.

Stephen Wiltshire

MEMORIES OF NEW YORK

It is our last day in New York and the end of our American adventure. Stephen suggests a picture of 'These are a few of my favourite things' as a valedictory greeting to marvellous Manhattan. Few drawings speak with such honest affection of a city that encapsulates his dreams. It is both touching and moving. For the child who was once locked within his own prisonhouse, unable to respond to others, rarely depicting them on paper, the female figure on the left of this drawing suggests a monumental development to a world where human relationships are seen as both possible and valuable.

Stephen has come a long way from the alienating landscape of his childhood.

Stephen Wiltshire

FINALE

In the space of seven months, Stephen has consumed his favourite cities and, lucky boy, preserved them intact in his internal visual lexicon. Endless days, months, years of pleasure lie ahead of him when he can summon up the remembered delights of these varied locations but, unlike the rest of us, Stephen will be able to walk in his head down Chicago's Michigan Avenue with a detailed and accurate map of the architectural landmarks on the blackboard of his mind. As he flies across the Grand Canyon in his helicopter, he will be able to reproduce the rock formations, and the scale and depth of this geological wonder without recourse to a photograph. The memory of the view down Park Avenue, culminating in the Pan-Am Building, is now immortalised on his internal screen, to be recalled instantly as his whim dictates. The twinkling fairy lights inside the stretch limo in New York, provided to fuel the richness of Stephen's dreams, will never be extinguished. A few bars of the theme music from *Rain Man* will remind him of the longed-for meeting with the composer in Santa Monica, and will trigger endless replay sequences to nurture his voracious appetite for the first Hollywood autistic hero, played by Dustin Hoffman.

Stephen's world is 'other' to our own. It is a self-contained pleasure palace of delights which provides constant private enjoyment. We glimpse his visions through the magic of his bewitching lines, marks on paper which transmute reality. Artistic endeavour is the highest manifestation of man and we who are not blessed with Stephen's rare, mysterious gift, are most fortunate to witness a miraculous phenomenon in an age which values and nurtures such genius. May future generations find inspiration in this unique boy to help others who will undoubtedly appear among us in the future.

The importance of education in the visual arts is central to the development of all children. May Stephen's drawings act as a beacon of enlightenment.